Animal Planet™
animalogy
weird & wacky animal facts

anim

weird &

al gy

vacky animal facts

By Rita Thievon Mullin

Illustrated by Anders Wenngren

Discovery Channel Publishing

Crown Publishers, Inc., New York

Published by Crown Publishers, Inc., a Random House company, 201 East 50th Street, New York, New York 10022

http://www.randomhouse.com/

CROWN is a trademark of Crown Publishers, Inc.

Printed in the United States of America

Library of Congress Cataloging-in-Publication Data
Mullin, Rita T.
Animalogy : weird & wacky animal facts / by Rita T. Mullin ; illustrated by Anders Wenngren
p. cm.
Includes index.
Summary: A collection of amazing facts about the animal world.
1. Animals—Miscellanea—Juvenile literature. [1. Animals—Miscellanea.] I. Wenngren, Anders, ill. II. Title.
QL49.M85 1997
590Ñdc21 97-29170

ISBN 0-517-80000-4 [pbk.]
0-517-80001-2 lib. bdg.]

Inspired by Animal Planet, the new cable television network from the people who bring you the Discovery Channel. For more information about Animal Planet's availability on your basic channel line-up, contact your cable or satellite company and visit our web site at *www.animal.discovery.com.*

For Michael
and Matthew

Art Director: David Cullen Whitmore
Editors: Kathy Ely, Maria Higgins

All photographs supplied by Bruce Coleman, Inc.

Credits from left to right are separated by semicolons, from top to bottom by dashes.

Cover: Michael Fogden — Mark Newman. Title page: Rod Williams. 6–7: Tom Brakefield. 8: Rod Williams. 9: Steve Solum. 10–11: Alan Blank. 12: Michael Fogden. 13: Kenneth W. Fink — K & K Ammann. 14: Tom Brakefield. 16: Rod Williams. 16–17: Joe McDonald. 18: Daniel J. Lyons. 19: Leonard Rue Jr. 20: Mark Newman. 22: E.R. Degginger. 23: Michael Fogden. 25: Mark Newman. 26–27: Frank Oberle. 28: Bob & Clara Calhoun. 30: Dwight Kuhn. 31: Kim Taylor. 32: Jeff Foott. 33: Ron & Valerie Taylor. 34: Michael Fogden. 35: Michael Fogden. 37: George D. Dodge. 38: Mark Newman. 41: Tui De Roy. 42: Erwin & Peggy Bauer. 43: Michael Fogden. 44–45: Tui De Roy. 47: John Shaw. 48–49: Jeff Foott; E.R. Degginger. 50: Tui De Roy. 51: Ron & Valerie Taylor. 53: George Marler. 54: Charles G. Summers. 55: Tui De Roy. 56: Reinhard Hans. 58: Melvin W. Larson. 59: Takacs Zoltan. 60: Joe McDonald. 61: Erwin & Peggy Bauer. 62: Norman Owen Tomalin. Back cover: K & K Ammann.

Contents

work that b

Animals fro

ody

eads to Tails

A Real Featherweight

The bald eagle, which measures more than three feet from head to tail and seven feet from wingtip to wingtip, weighs only about nine pounds. In fact, its feathers weigh twice as much as its hollow skeleton. Those air-filled bones let it maneuver suddenly in the air and ride on thermals to save energy, and they give the eagle the lift it needs to take off even with sizable prey in its beak or talons.

Unbelievable Bodies

Pass the Hippo Oil ▶

A hippopotamus spends its life naked in the sun and never burns. That's because of the reddish "lotion" that oozes from the hippo's skin—a substance that scientists have found works great on human skin, too.

▲ Peacock Brown?!?

Those beautiful, iridescent peacock feathers are really brown. Each feather is made up of thin, grooved layers of keratin, the same material found in nails and hair. The grooves catch and bend the light into colors like those on a soap bubble—or an oil slick.

Let Me Feel Your Muscles

The average person has 696 muscles, but a single caterpillar has more than 4,000.

Shocking!

The charge released by an electric eel is powerful enough to start 50 cars.

Unbelievable Bodies

Doing Your Scales

The pangolin, or scaly anteater, is the only mammal with scales. This covering is made of keratin, the same material that makes up horns and hooves. While the scales on its foot-long body are rounded, the scales on its two-foot-long tail are razor-sharp to protect it from attackers.

Kung Fu Kangaroo ▶

In a fight, a kangaroo can balance on its tail to kick with both powerful hind legs at the same time.

BIG DEAL

Largest mammal	**Blue whale**	100 feet
Largest reptile	**Anaconda**	33 feet
Largest fish	**Whale shark**	50 feet
Largest bird	**Ostrich**	9 feet
Largest amphibian	**Chinese giant salamander**	6 feet
Largest insect	**Stick insect**	1.7 feet

SMALL WORLD

Smallest mammal	**Etruscan shrew**	1.25 inches
Smallest reptile	**Monito gecko lizard**	1.50 inches
Smallest fish	**Pygmy dwarf goby**	.30 inches
Smallest bird	**Bee hummingbird**	2.25 inches
Smallest amphibian	**Brazilian gold frog**	.39 inches
Smallest insect	**Fairy fly**	.0084 inches

Unbelievable Bodies

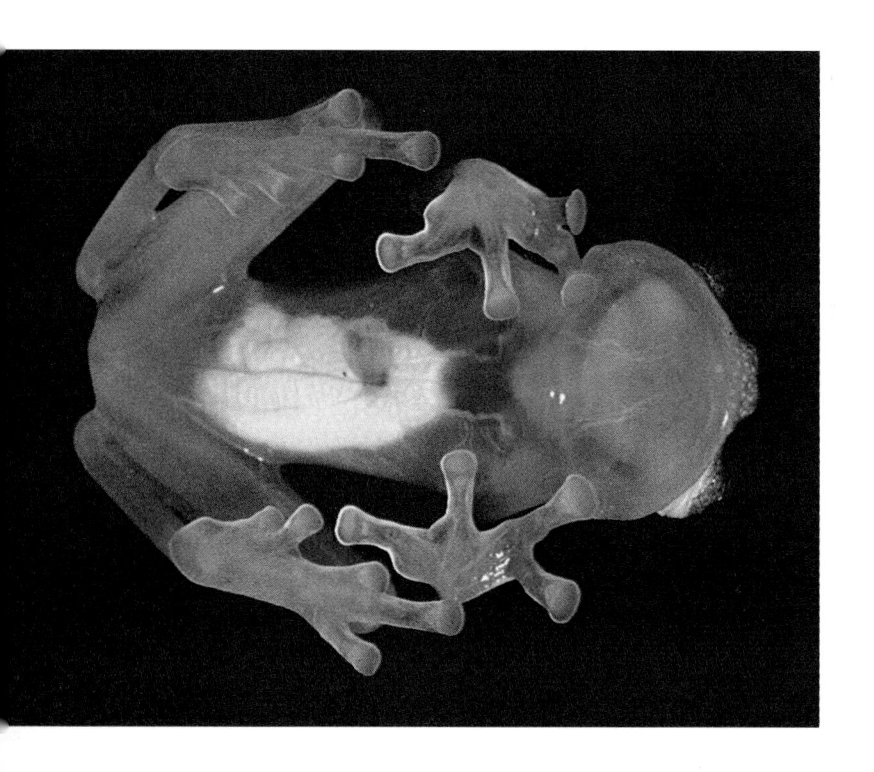

Built-In Straw
An elephant's trunk—really a nose and an upper lip—has more than 100,000 muscles. It's strong enough to uproot a tree, yet agile enough to pick up a single blade of grass. But its everyday job is to be a straw. The trunk typically sucks up two to three gallons of water at a time and sprays it into the elephant's mouth. A thirsty pachyderm can drink 56 gallons of water this way in less than five minutes.

◀ **Peekaboo Parts**
The skin on the lower body of the bare-hearted glass frog of South America is translucent, showing its beating heart and other organs.

Blood Bath
A giraffe's heart pumps 16 gallons of blood a minute—enough to fill a bathtub in only three minutes.

Fangs for the Memories
The gaboon viper is the snake with the longest fangs—they stretch nearly two inches.

◀ Tail Lights

Zebras' stripes may look similar from the side, but from the rear each zebra species has unique markings. All the better to follow one another on long journeys across the African plains.

▲ Vroom, Vroom

Don't ever drag-race with a cheetah. Like a fine sports car, it can go from 0 to 55 mph in only three seconds.

High Jumper

A flea accelerates 50 times faster than the space shuttle—and it can jump more than 100 times its own height. That would be like a six-foot-tall man leaping over a 40-story building.

The Eye Is Quicker Than the Hand

Thanks in part to its complex eyes, a housefly can react to a swat 10 times faster than a hand can make the move.

FAST, FASTER, FASTEST

Fastest animal in water	**Sailfish**	68 mph
Fastest animal on land	**Cheetah**	70 mph
Fastest animal in the air	**Peregrine falcon**	200 mph

Can't Catch Me

The pronghorn, which speeds across North American grasslands at more than 60 miles per hour, is the fastest animal in the Western Hemisphere. While outrunning predators, this deer cousin raises its tail to reveal a white rump, flashing a danger signal to pronghorns as far as a mile or more away.

▼ Bet on Bigfoot

If an ostrich and a thoroughbred horse were sprinting, the ostrich, clocked at 40 miles per hour, would take the prize. It runs on its two toes (and, incidentally, can kick with 500 pounds of power per square inch). The joint halfway up the ostrich's leg isn't a backward-bending knee—it's an ankle. Everything below is the rest of its foot.

Animal Athletes

Pumping Iron
An ant can carry 50 times its body weight. That would be the same as a man toting a rhinoceros around on his back.

◀ Winner by a Nose
The proboscis monkey of Borneo has not only a world-class nose but a prize-winning freestyle stroke. It is one of the best swimming primates, and it spends much of its time in or near water. Groups of them have even been seen "vacationing" in the ocean waves.

Jump Back
The jackrabbit can cover more than 12 feet in one hop—and can clear a five-foot-tall obstacle in its path of escape from coyotes, foxes, or eagles.

Beep! Beep!
Although Africa's green mamba snakes live mostly in trees, they can move so quickly across the ground that they have been known to kick up a cloud of dust as they speed across the savanna.

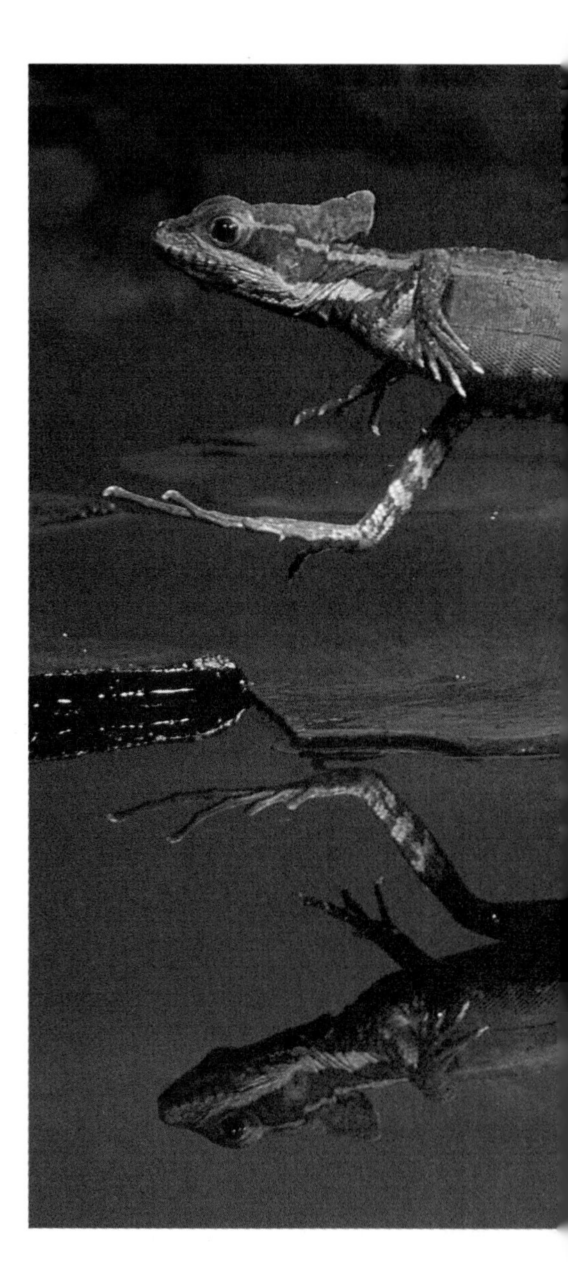

It's a Miracle

The basilisk lizard, popularly called the Jesus lizard, can "walk on water" by moving its legs quickly and dropping down special scaly flaps on its toes.

Baby Face

You're Grounded
A newborn giraffe is born into the school of hard knocks. It can fall five feet from its mother's womb to the ground below. The shock of the fall starts its breathing.

Tailgating
When a mother shrew heads out, her youngsters line up behind her, each biting the tail of the shrew in front of it.

Ouch!
The flightless kiwi lays from one to three eggs each season. Each egg weighs about 25 percent of the mother's total body weight—comparable to an average woman giving birth to a 35-pound baby. Lucky for her, the male incubates the eggs for about 80 days—maybe to give her a chance to rest.

Missing Link?
South America's hoatzin chicks are born with claws on their wings, like those found on fossils of the archaeopteryx, a prehistoric ancestor of the bird.

◀ **Nasty Newborn**

From the moment the Indian cobra pokes its head from its leathery egg, its venom is as lethal as an adult's.

Hide-and-Seek

Although a fawn is vulnerable to attack during its first wobbly days, its spotted coat helps it blend in with its surroundings, concealing it from wily predators. In a few weeks, when the fawn can run rather than hide from danger, its spots disappear.

Baby Face

Backpackin' Mama
What's a mother to do? You live in a tree, but your unborn tadpoles must remain in water. The pygmy marsupial frog has one solution: She carries her eggs in fluid-filled sacs on her back.

▼ A Whale of a Mother
A mother beluga whale will tenderly turn on her side and carry a newborn to the surface to take its first breath. If the baby dies, she will try to revive it, often pushing it ahead of her through the water.

Sing for Your Supper
Baby polar bears often hum as they nurse on their mother's milk.

Stop Her Before She Breeds Again
One tiny female white aphid can produce an army of aphids to wreck your rose garden without any help from the male of the species, thank you. In a single season a female's direct descendants can exceed six billion—all exact clones of the first.

Sibling Rivalry
Even in the womb, the sand shark is a fierce predator. The developing embryos feed on each other until typically only two remain to be born.

Well-Balanced Baby
A goat antelope, born on high mountain ledges, is cruising over rocky ridges behind Mom within hours of birth.

Run, Baby, Run
A two-day-old gazelle can outrun an adult horse.

▼ **Day-Care Center**

Organized day care is nothing new in the animal world. Flamingos, penguins, meerkats, giraffes—even crocodiles—leave their youngsters with other parents or relatives while they head out to find food.

I Can't Hear You—My Legs Are Crossed
A cricket hears through special organs located on its front legs.

Sweet Smell of Success
The kiwi, a flightless bird that lives on a diet primarily of earthworms, has nostrils on the end of its long bill. It can sniff out worms below ground and then use its bill to dig in for dinner.

◀ Owl Get Ya
From its midnight hunting perch, the barn owl can hear the tiniest movements—and even the breathing—of a mouse quivering in a field.

You Look Hot
The rattlesnake is equipped with two pits just below its eyes that "see" even subtle changes in air temperature before it. The rattler uses that sense to detect and strike at warm-blooded prey.

Pardon Me—No, Pardon Me
Several different badger families often share their labyrinthine burrows. They get along just fine by recognizing each family's unique scent, appearance, and sounds—and giving each other a wide berth.

▼ **The Better to Smell You with, My Dear**

The male atlas moth can smell a female up to seven miles away—and it doesn't even have a nose. Its fernlike antennae can detect a single molecule of the female's scent in the air.

If You're So Smart...

Author, Author!
Scientists are teaching some chimpanzees to use computers with special buttons that type words so the chimps can talk not only to trainers, but to other people—and even to each other.

Forget Roach Motel—Try Roach University
Cockroaches can be taught to run a maze successfully. Scientists rigged complicated pathways leading to a jelly-glass "home." After five or six tries, most of the roaches had reduced their time running the maze—and by the end of the day many were doing it without making any mistakes. Some still remembered the next day.

Little Drummer Bird
The black palm cockatoo of Australia doesn't just sing to let other birds know it has claimed its territory. It accompanies itself by breaking off a stick and banging it on a hollow tree.

Toolin' Around
Humans and apes aren't the only animals to use tools. The Galápagos Islands' woodpecker finch feeds on grubs in dead wood, but it lacks a true woodpecker's long tongue to reach the tasty treats. Instead, it grabs a nearby wood splinter or cactus spine to probe a hole until its dinner is in reach. And the Egyptian vulture drops stones on eggs that are too large to crack with its beak.

▼ Can You Open This Jar for Me?
When a crab enclosed in a jar is placed before an octopus, the octopus will soon surround the glass with its tentacles and try to pull off the top—even unscrewing the lid.

Yeah, but How Good Are They at Algebra?

Gorillas that have been given IQ tests in sign language have scored 85 to 95. The average human's IQ score is 100.

behave you

animal

rself

o the strangest things

Jungle Gym

Sometimes bears just want to have fun. One researcher watched as two black bear cubs discovered that a young tree bent to the ground under the weight of both of them would send one flying through the air if the other hopped off. The cubs spent the rest of the afternoon catapulting each other through the trees.

On the Move

Are We There Yet?
The Arctic tern holds the world record for migratory travel. Each year it flies from its Arctic Circle nesting grounds to feeding sites off Antarctica and back—a round trip of 22,000 miles.

Long Way Home
The green sea turtle journeys nearly 1,400 miles from the Brazilian coast to Ascension Island in the mid-Atlantic each year to lay its eggs. Scientists who tagged young turtles born on the island found that they not only returned to the island but to the *exact same shore* when they were ready to breed.

▲ Some Vacation
The rufous hummingbird (above), which is less than four inches long, travels from its Alaskan breeding ground to Mexico each year—a 6,000-mile round trip. The ruby-throated hummingbird crosses the Gulf of Mexico each breeding season—a 500-mile nonstop journey.

Extreme Parasailing
A young spider can catch the wind with homemade "sails" it produces by bending down and releasing silk from its abdomen. Soon the breeze catches the silk, and the spider floats away. Ships hundreds of miles from land have encountered these tiny balloonists.

Someone's Been Sleeping in My Tree

The millions of monarch butterflies that blanket trees in their autumn mating grounds in Mexico, Florida, California, and Texas are great-great-grandchildren of butterflies that left there the previous spring. How does the new generation of butterflies find its way back to mating grounds they've never visited before? Researchers think that the butterflies' sense of smell leads them toward the scent still lingering there from the previous fall.

KEEPIN' THE BEAT

Hummingbirds may have the fastest wing speed of all birds, but they're slowpokes compared to some insects.

Animal	Beats per second
Hummingbird	78
Fruit fly	250
Mosquito	600
Midge	1,000

◀ **Hut, Two, Three, Four**

When army ants go on a hunt, they march for weeks without breaking formation—six to eight perfect columns that stretch for hundreds of yards. When they receive chemical signals from the leader ants telling them they've found prey, they swarm and attack.

Hunt and Peck

▲ *Thwick!*

The chameleon's tongue, its main weapon in hunting insects, takes less than a hundredth of a second to reach its prey.

Do the Stomp

The North American wood turtle stamps its feet on the ground to drive shaken earthworms to the surface—and into its waiting mouth.

Poison Spitball

The spitting cobra of Africa can shoot its poison more than six feet, blinding any enemy that dares to disturb it.

Use Your Fork, Dear

The japyx, a simple, underground insect that looks like a worm, comes armed with its own utensils. Its back end is equipped with a two-pronged tail that looks and acts like a fork. When hunting its tiny insect prey, the japyx backs into a narrow passage and grabs its dinner between the prongs. The japyx then brings its built-in fork around to its mouth.

Fatal Firefly

The female of one firefly species preys on the male of another species that produces natural chemicals to ward off insect eaters. She tricks the unsuspecting male by responding to its mating call with the call of the female of his species. When he lands to mate, she eats him and stores the toxins to protect herself.

Spittin' Distance
The archer fish can spit drops of water as far as five feet to shoot insects off overhanging leaves. It even corrects its aim to allow for the way water bends the light.

Hunt and Peck

▲ **Swim -Through Window**

The sea otter likes to eat on the move. It floats on its back, balancing a flat rock on its tummy, and uses it to crack open the shellfish it scoops from the sea.

DEADLY DOZEN

Sure, lots of snakes have venom. But they aren't the only critters with a killer bite. Here's a list of the most venomous examples of each animal:

MOST VENOMOUS	NAME	LOCATION
Coral	Fire coral	Florida, Caribbean
Fish	Stonefish	Indo-Pacific region
Frog	Golden poison frog	South America
Hydrozoa	Portuguese man-of-war	Tropical oceans
Insect	Afrur	Sinai desert
Jellyfish	Sea wasp	Australia, Philippines
Lizard	Gila monster	North America
◀ Octopus	Blue-ringed octopus	Australia
Shellfish	Cone shell	Worldwide
Snake	Many-banded krait	China, Burma
Spider	Black widow spider	North America
Toad	Marine toad	South America

Sting Operation ▶

Bees aren't immune to their own venom. Warring queen honeybees will engage in fatal stinging battles.

Reel 'em In

The cone shell shoots out a poisonous, jagged harpoon that kills its prey. Then it reels it in to eat. If the fish breaks free, the shell shoots out a second dart. The harpoon may stretch a distance five times longer than the shell itself.

You're Not Having ME for Dinner

Best Performance as a Corpse
The West Indian wood snake could teach the opossum something about playing dead. When a predator nears, it lies still as its eyes fill with blood and blood drools from its mouth.

▼ Pretty Poison
South America's colorful arrow poison frogs pack a deadly wallop. An ounce of one species' poison could kill 2 1/2 *million* people. Their bright colors warn predators to give them a wide berth. Their popular name comes from natives' use of their secretions on darts. A single tiny frog's venom coats 50 poison darts.

Dinner Didn't Agree with Me
The sharp-ribbed newt of eastern Asia gets its revenge on a predator that takes a bite. The amphibian's spiked ribs pierce the attacker's skin, injecting painful poison into its mouth. The newt often gets spit back out to safety.

I Am My Own Worst Enemy
The chameleon can change its color completely as light and temperature change. But occasionally its emotions get in the way. An angry chameleon darkens, and a fearful one turns nearly white—making it stand out against its environment when under attack.

Moon Eyes
One South American frog, *Physalaemus nattereri*, has huge eye spots on its rump. When a predator approaches, the frog turns around and lifts up its back end, revealing the huge "eyes." If the predator still keeps coming, the frog greets it with a stinky secretion that usually sends it on its way.

▼ What a Frill

The frill-necked lizard stands on its hind legs, extends its enormous, colorful frills, and opens its wide mouth to frighten off predators in a fake attack. The frills also come in handy for scaring off rivals and impressing females.

You're Not Having ME for Dinner

▼ Next Time, Order Chicken

A shark that swallows a spine-covered sea hedgehog is eating its last meal. Once inside the shark's stomach, the sea hedgehog inflates, and its sharp needles rip a hole in the shark's side that becomes the hedgehog's escape hatch—and the shark's fatal wound.

No Thanks, I Just Ate

The West African swallowtail caterpillar's color and shape resemble a bird dropping. If that's not enough to send a curious predator packing, further contact produces a stink-bomb secretion.

Here's Mace in Your Face

When attacked, the bombardier beetle lets out a loud pop and spurts a boiling, irritating spray directly at its attacker, startling and stinging its enemy with one fell swoop.

Stop Lights

Fireflies' flashing signals would seem to make them easy targets, but several species are also equipped with toxins that spiders and birds quickly learn to avoid.

Tail of Woe

Many reptiles can grow a new tail if they lose one to a predator. But a Barber's skink goes even further. Its brightly colored back end attracts unwary predators—who end up with a parting gift while the less noticeable rest of the skink slips away unharmed.

▼ Snake Eyes

One species of South American sphinx caterpillar, which looks just like a twig when it is resting on a branch, surprises attackers by inflating its front end into a miniature snake head—complete with realistic-looking snake eyes. It will even strike at anything that touches it.

Talk to Me

Ocean Opera

During mating season, male humpback whales sing elaborate songs that can last half an hour or longer—the most complicated songs sung by any animal. Their tunes can travel for miles underwater. All humpbacks in a single ocean sing the same song during a season—and learn a new song each year. Their music has been measured at 100 decibels—the same volume as a pneumatic drill. But the honor of loudest animal goes to the blue whale, whose sounds measure 188 decibels—as loud as a rocket launch.

Go Three Blocks, Turn Left . . .
When a honeybee finds a great stash of nectar, it shares the wealth. Back at the hive, it gives free samples of the fluid, dances in a figure eight, and flutters its wings so fast that they buzz. The direction it faces when dancing tells the other bees which way to head, and its speed lets them know how far to travel—the faster the dance, the farther the feast.

Let's Get Ready to Rumble
Elephants call across the savanna using sounds below the range that humans can hear—but for elephants these sounds are as loud as a rock band in your living room. Their voices can carry more than two miles.

Rat-a-Tattoo
When a kangaroo rat chooses a patch of grass to munch, it taps out its signature song with its feet, warning others to keep their distance.

Copycat Bird
The marsh warbler steals songs from anyone it can. One of these mimics can perform tunes from 200 different species of birds from Europe to Africa.

▼ Make Your Own Kind of Music

Scientists used to think that birds of the same species had distinct, recognizable songs. But now they've learned that birds of the same species that live in different regions sing different songs. For example, male wrens in Oregon sing 30 different songs, but their New York cousins sing only two.

Boy Meets Girl

▼ **Alligator Love**

When ready to mate, male and female alligators chase each other in circles so violently that fish go flying from the pond and frogs stop singing.

Who's Your Decorator?
A male bowerbird wouldn't build just any shady lair to attract interested females. Some paint the inside with berry juice, others decorate with colorful stones and shiny objects, and still others mix a plaster of burnt wood and saliva to cover the bower's inside walls.

Dinner Date
Lynx couples, like many other large cats, will hunt together for several days before mating. The hunting gives the female a chance to be sure that she's mating with the most dominant cat on the range—if he isn't, he'll soon be sent running by Mr. Big.

Sumo Seals
Male elephant seals stage elaborate wrestling matches to earn the right to mate with the females.

Scrambled Eggs
In one region of the North Sea, 50 million plaice gather each season to lay their eggs. Total number of eggs laid by these fish in one season: more than eight trillion! Currents carry the eggs to points south.

Single Birds' Bar
During breeding time, female great frigatebirds take the lead in finding mates. Males perch on bushes, and as females "cruise by," each male inflates its bright red neck pouch and flaps its wings wildly to attract a female to come to his side to mate.

You Are Feeling Very Sleepy

Neck Napper
Giraffes only need to sleep deeply for 20 minutes each night. Most of the time they're half awake, alert to any danger.

▼ Fish Yawn?!?
Yup. So do birds, reptiles, and amphibians—as well as mammals. And yawning is just as contagious for animals as for humans. When ostriches settle down for the night, the highest-ranking birds yawn first, followed by the rest of the flock. This way, they settle down together and are ready to awaken to feed together the next day—to another chorus of yawns.

Half Asleep
The beluga whale sleeps with one eye open—and half its brain awake—to keep alert to danger and to come to the surface occasionally to breathe. Partway through its nap, the sides of its brain—and its eyes—switch, allowing it to rest completely without ever being fully asleep.

Beautiful Dreamers
Researchers have found that cats and dogs—in fact, all mammals—experience Rapid Eye Movement, or REM sleep, the period when the brain is highly active and the eyes dart around beneath the lids. Since REM sleep is the period during which humans dream, chances are good that Fido is chasing Puff during his nap as well.

A Long Winter's Nap
Before settling down to hibernate, bears consume as much as 20,000 calories a day to live on through the winter. Once they settle down, they may sleep for up to seven months. Unlike smaller animals, which drop their body temperatures dramatically when hibernating, bears reduce theirs by only a few degrees.

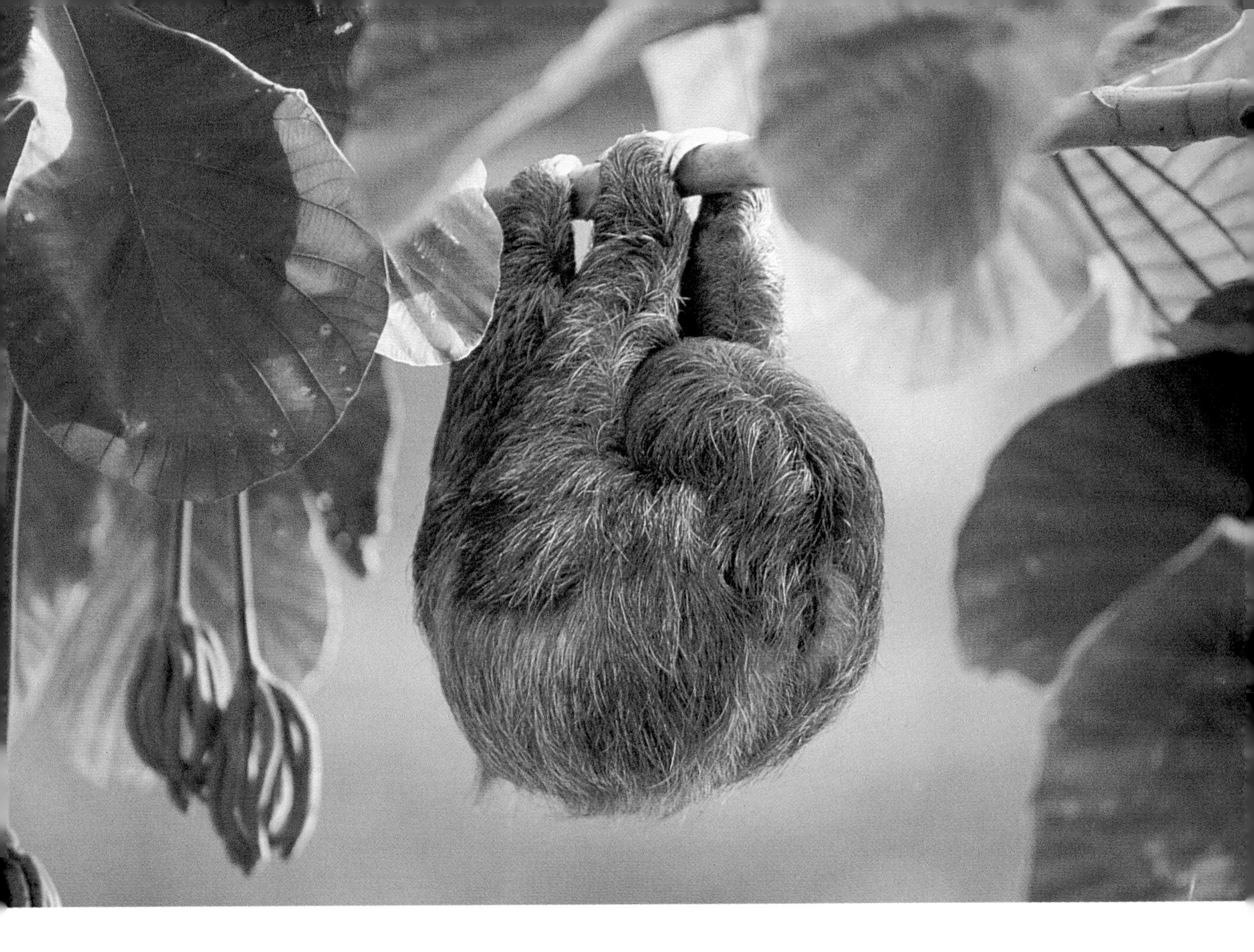

▲ Just Let Me Sleep a Little More

Sloths, which live in the humid rain forest canopy, sleep up to 20 hours a day. And when they're awake, they move so little that their gray-brown fur has a distinct green cast from the algae that grows there.

home, swe

amazing anim

Popeye the Sailor Iguana

The marine iguana of the Galápagos Islands is the world's only seagoing lizard. To withstand the cold ocean water, this cold-blooded creature first warms itself on rocks before it dives in to grab a bite of seaweed dinner.

t home

eighborhoods

Nice Nest You've Got There

Sold!
Spring is house-hunting season all over. Male robins fly north ahead of the females to scope out safe nesting spots. The chorus that greets the dawn each spring is made up of males staking their claims against interlopers.

Houseboat
The grebe, a water bird related to the loon, not only spends most of its life in the water, it builds its nest there, constructing a floating pontoon of vegetation that it hides among the water plants.

Just a Little Freshening Up
Starlings often return to old nests. But to protect newborns from infection, the parents line the recycled home with plants that are toxic to microorganisms and insects. Only then does the female lay her eggs. The birds continue to add fresh shoots while minding their offspring.

Great Wall of Mud
Hornbills not only hide their nests inside hollow tree trunks, they wall up the opening with mud made from soil and saliva. The father leaves a hole large enough to pass through food. As the chicks grow and need more food, the mother breaks through the protection to help in the search for sustenance. The stay-at-home babies build the wall back up until her return.

◀ All Sewn Up
Using thin fibers resembling thread, the Indian tailorbird sews together two close-growing leaves to form a nest pocket. It then fills the pouch with cottony down before laying its eggs inside.

◀ **Room for Rent—A.C. Included**

Termite mounds in the African savanna can tower over 25 feet high and measure 40 feet around. The mounds also come equipped with air conditioning: fungi "gardens" inside absorb excess moisture and give off heat as they grow, providing a constant level of temperature and humidity.

Underground

Diet of Worms

The Australian earthworm can grow up to eight feet long. Pulling one out of its burrow can require two men, but natives consider it worth the struggle: it's a tasty delicacy.

▼ **Splitting Headache**

Most species of skink,a kind of lizard, have developed a pointed "drill head" for burrowing underground. Some species' eyes are permanently closed to keep out flying dirt.

Gopher Broke

Gophers usually live happily on plant roots, but some of these burrowing critters in the Midwestern states have discovered a new treat—telephone cables. They dig three feet below the surface and chow down on the lead in the wires, breaking into transcontinental calls with regularity. To dissuade these underground operators, phone repairers now cover the wires with less tasty steel tape.

Shut the Door!

The trap-door spider stays inside its hole in the ground all day, protected by a self-closing door with a hinge of spider silk. When night falls, the door opens slowly and the spider waits at the entrance for unsuspecting insects to pass. When one makes that fatal mistake, the spider quickly drags its prey inside as the door slams shut behind it.

Mud Bath

The springtail, an almost microscopic soil-dwelling insect, insists on staying clean despite its dirty home. It oozes out a drop of cleaning fluid from its mouth onto a front claw and rubs it over its head, antennae, and legs. It completes its bath by passing the drop back to the second pair of legs to clean the rest. No waste here, though: the springtail swallows the remainder, saving the solution for its next bathtime.

Old Man Cicada ▶

Cicadas, popularly known as 17-year locusts, are the world's longest-living insects, but they spend only a few weeks of their lives aboveground, when they mate and lay eggs in the soil for the next generation.

▲ How About a Brisk Swim Instead?

One of only three birds that use their paddle-like wings rather than webbed feet to propel themselves through the water (the others are auks and petrels), penguins can move steadily at three to six mph and sprint at up to 15. Unlike most water birds, penguins not only catch their prey underwater, they often eat it there.

War in Slow-Mo

Sea anemones look more like plants than animals, yet they do move—at a pace you'd hardly notice, about an inch an hour. But when an alien anemone invades another's turf, look out. Each brings out the big guns: poison-tipped harpoons usually reserved for catching fish. They shoot until one surrenders, beating a very s-l-o-w retreat.

Water, Water Everywhere

Ptooey!

The whale shark, at 50 feet and four to five tons, is the world's largest fish. It reaches its enormous size on a diet of shrimplike plankton and schools of small fish. Like a giant underwater vacuum cleaner, it sucks up about 2,000 tons of water per hour, along with anything in its path, including pieces of driftwood and old shoes.

▶

All Zipped Up

The yapok, a nocturnal marsupial, spends so much time in the water feeding on crabs and fish that its pouch has a watertight muscle across the opening.

Glow Away!

Instead of spraying black ink at attackers like their cousins in the upper ocean, several octopus species that live in the deepest and darkest ocean regions produce a chemical cloud that glows, surprising the predator while the octopus slips away into the blackness.

Water, Water Everywhere

Bottoms Up

Most fish have lighter colors on their underside so they blend in with the light when viewed from below. They are darker on top to blend in better with underwater plants and mud when seen from above. But the Nile catfish, which swims upside down to keep an eye on the plants growing on the water's surface, reverses the trend: its belly is dark, and its back is lighter.

▼ Here's Bug in Your Eye

The flashlight fish attracts plankton with a light it projects from pockets below its eyes. It can also roll the pockets in and out to blink the light off and on, confusing potential predators. The light is produced by glowing bacteria that live in the pouches and feed off nutrients in the fish's blood.

Taken to the Cleaners

The sea swallow, a fish living in Pacific coral reefs, survives on parasites it cleans off larger fish. This "cleaner fish" is brightly colored to advertise its services to "customer fish," who approach it for a clean sweep.

Life in the (Deep Sea) Trenches

No mouth, no guts, no problem. The giant tube worm can still eat thanks to a bacteria that lives within its body. The bacteria feeds on chemicals in the water and gives off a kind of sugar that feeds the tube worm.

A Light Meal

The angler fish, which lives in the murky depths beyond the sun's reach, lures its prey with a light attached to a line that dangles in front of its mouth.

Poof!

Sea dandelions, corals related to jellyfish, release eight-armed polyps that look and act like dandelion puffs. They drift slowly along in the water before landing on the seafloor to bud, creating new coral.

The Lion's Mane Inn

The lion's mane jellyfish provides a safe haven for young jackfish, who are immune to its tentacles' venom. In return, the brightly colored fish attract unwary predators, who quickly become prey as they are swept up to be eaten by the jellyfish.

What Do You Mean, It's Cold?

▲ Winter Clothes

The ptarmigan is one of only a handful of birds that remain in the North throughout the winter. Each fall it grows feathers on its feet that act as snowshoes and trades its brown feathers for white ones. During a bad storm, the ptarmigan will burrow into a snowbank for protection. In the spring, the shoes come off and its warm weather feathers emerge once again.

Ice on the Wing

While many life forms died during the last Ice Age, a butterfly that can still be found in Scandinavia survived. Its larvae consumed what little vegetation it was buried with and emerged when the glaciers subsided.

Keepin' Cozy

The Arctic ground squirrel survives the long, cold winter in surprising comfort. To prepare for its nine-month-long hibernation, it builds its burrow in a well-drained hillside so that ice won't form inside, and it chooses a location where snow will drift to insulate the den. It also digs the entrance below most of the den, so that its rising body heat is trapped inside.

Polar Litterers

Lemmings are the only Arctic animals that mate year-round. And since a single female can deliver seven litters of up to eight pups each during a year, lemming communities can increase a hundredfold each season. Lemmings multiply so quickly that the Alaskan Eskimos' name for them translates as "the ones that fell from the sky." These rodents' large numbers—and large appetites (each must consume up to twice its weight in food each day)—have a dramatic impact on Arctic plant life.

Winter White

The polar bear's signature white coat is actually made up of clear, hollow hairs that trap ultraviolet light and conduct it to the bear's skin, where it is changed to heat. The fur also keeps heat from escaping: scientists trying to track bears from the air using infrared photography to spot heat coming off bodies can't see them. Their fur insulates so well that it holds in 95 percent of the animals' warmth.

What Do You Mean, It's Cold?

◀ Turning Winter on Its Head

The bison, or buffalo, takes prairie winters head-on—literally. When fierce storms tear across the grasslands, the bison lowers its shaggy head and stands facing into the wind, protected by an extra supply of fur on its head and shoulders.

Don't Bug Me

Although caribou and reindeer are preyed on by eagles, bears, and wolves, their worst enemies are insects. During the summer months, mosquitoes can suck up to four ounces of blood from an animal in a single day. In fall, warble flies lay their eggs on the beasts' leg hair; their larvae then drill into the deer's flesh to develop. And nose botflies lay eggs in the animals' nostrils in the fall to winter over inside their nose and throat—as the poor hosts unsuccessfully try to cough and sneeze the developing larvae out into the cold. Full-grown flies emerge from their nostrils and mouths in the spring, and the whole nasty business starts again.

Down Comforter

To withstand the Antarctic winter, where temperatures can reach minus 75 degrees Fahrenheit, penguins rely on several overlapping layers of waterproof feathers to hold in their body heat.

▼ Built-In Antifreeze

One mite found in Antarctica survives the winter by producing glycerol, a chemical similar to the one used in automobile antifreeze.

Dry as Dust

▲ No Thanks, I've Got My Canteen

A desert tortoise can store up to a pint of water—a season's supply—in sacs beneath its shell.

Water? Nah, Never Touch the Stuff
Kangaroo rats and prairie dogs never drink water. Their bodies get all the fluids they need from the desert plants they eat.

The Ears Have It
The North American jackrabbit's oversize ears are equipped with large arteries near the surface to release body heat, keeping the critter cool. On chilly nights, its ears also act as a built-in blanket, covering its back.

Sharp, Yet Satisfying
The javelina, a desert pig, dines comfortably on cholla and prickly-pear cactus—which supply both food and drink. The pig simply rips off and spits out the largest spines and chews up the smaller ones to reach the pulp.

◀ **Love You, Honeypot**
Some honeypot ants serve as living storage tanks for their colony. They eat until their elastic abdomens are filled with honeydew and then they stay in the nest, available to feed the others if outside food stores dry up.

Dry Nose and Throat

Snakes that live in the desert sand have valves that close off their nostrils when the reptile dives through a dune.

Forecast: Hot and Humid

▲ No Drowned Rat

The Amazon's 100-pound capybara, the world's largest rodent, spends so much time in the river that it can swim better than it can walk.

Ah, a Breath of Fresh Air
During the Amazon's dry season, the mighty river is reduced to a trickle and many of its tributaries are no more than a few isolated ponds. Many fish there have had to adapt air-breathing techniques to survive. The electric eel absorbs oxygen through a lining in its mouth, and the pirarucu (at 14 feet long and 440 pounds, the world's largest freshwater fish) survives by surfacing every 15 minutes or so to breathe through its lunglike swim bladder.

Finger Food
The rain forest of Madagascar is home to the aye-aye, a rare rabbit-size primate that scrambles through the forest canopy. Each front foot has a long, thin finger that extends far beyond the rest of its digits, allowing it to poke grubs out of trees once it chews off a section of outer bark.
On the ground it uses its fingers to pry the meat from nuts it opens with its razor-sharp incisors.

Beak Beak!
The toucan's beak can be as long as the rest of the bird's body. Despite the beak's impressive size, it has lots of air holes, which make it surprisingly light. Each beak has a unique pattern, giving fellow toucans a way to recognize one another at a distance.

Works Better Than a Textbook
Rainy season? No problem. Orangutans make umbrellas out of branches and large leaves to protect themselves from downpours.

Leaf Us Alone
The Amazon River has so few food sources in it that fish survive on shore plants that fall into the water. And one fish, the arowhana, leaps from the water to grab insects or spiders from overhanging branches.

Flood Insurance

Each summer, when the Amazon submerges trees 30 feet tall, it's business as usual for the uakari, a plucky little monkey that lives in the rain forest canopy. Its leafy penthouse shields it not only from the flooding but from the region's most deadly predators—jaguars and eagles. And its face protects it from native people, who would rather hunt something that doesn't look quite so human.

Up on the Roof

The loris, a kind of lemur, doesn't take any chances. When it crawls across its rain forest canopy home, it always makes sure it's holding on to a limb with at least three legs. Its slow, cautious speed lets it creep up on its nighttime prey without being noticed.

What Goes Around Comes Around

When the Amazon recedes, the vicious piranhas (scourges of prey from small fish to capybaras as large as 100 pounds) finally meet their match. Isolated in pools, these groups of aquatic killers quickly diminish the food supply and become ready prey themselves: the four-foot-long giant otter grabs the fish with its forepaws and takes a bite out of crime with its powerful jaws.

How Dry I Am

The Amazon's tarantula, a large, hairy spider that can measure 10 inches across from leg to leg, can survive without water for nearly three months of the region's hottest, driest season.

▼ Eat Your Heart Out, Flipper

Amazon catfish aren't the least bit fazed by the dry season. When the river narrows, they simply pull themselves along the muddy ground with their pectoral fins.

Index